Popular Rock Superstars
POP ROCK

AC/DC	**Elton John**
Aerosmith	**The Grateful Dead**
The Allman Brothers Band	**Led Zeppelin**
	Lynyrd Skynyrd
The Beatles	**Pink Floyd**
Billy Joel	**Queen**
Bob Marley and the Wailers	**The Rolling Stones**
Bruce Springsteen	**U2**
The Doors	**The Who**

The Doors

Rae Simons

Mason Crest Publishers

The Doors

FRONTIS Though their career together was brief, Ray Manzarek, Jim Morrison, Robby Krieger, and John Densmore (clockwise from top left) had a major impact on the rock world.

Produced by 21st Century Publishing and Communications, Inc.

Editorial by Harding House Publishing Services, Inc.

Copyright © 2008 by Mason Crest Publishers. All rights reserved. No part of this publication may be reproduced or transmitted in any form or by any means, electronic or mechanical, including photocopying, recording, taping, or any information storage and retrieval system, without permission from the publisher.

MASON CREST PUBLISHERS INC.
370 Reed Road
Broomall, Pennsylvania 19008
(866) MCP-BOOK (toll free)
www.masoncrest.com

Printed in the United States.

First Printing

9 8 7 6 5 4 3 2 1

Library of Congress Cataloging-in-Publication Data

Simons, Rae, 1957–
   The Doors / Rae Simons.
     p. cm. — (Popular rock superstars of yesterday and today)
   Includes bibliographical references and index.
   Hardback edition: ISBN-13: 978-1-4222-0190-9
   Paperback edition: ISBN-13: 978-1-4222-0312-5
 1. Doors (Musical group)—Juvenile literature. 2. Rock musicians—United States—Juvenile literature. I. Title.
ML3930.D66S56 2008
782.42166092'2—dc22
[B]
                                                2007019388

Publisher's notes:
- All quotations in this book come from original sources, and contain the spelling and grammatical inconsistencies of the original text.
- The Web sites mentioned in this book were active at the time of publication. The publisher is not responsible for Web sites that have changed their addresses or discontinued operation since the date of publication. The publisher will review and update the Web site addresses each time the book is reprinted.

CONTENTS

	Rock 'n' Roll Timeline	6
1	**Blast from the Past**	9
2	**The Beginning**	15
3	**Finding Fame**	21
4	**Drugs, Destruction, and Death**	33
5	**After Jim**	45
	Chronology	56
	Accomplishments & Awards	58
	Further Reading & Internet Resources	60
	Glossary	61
	Index	62
	Picture Credits	64
	About the Author	64

Rock 'n' Roll Timeline

1950s

1951 — "Rocket 88," considered by many to be the first rock single, is released by Ike Turner.

1952 — DJ Alan Freed coins and popularizes the term "Rock and Roll," proclaimes himself the "Father of Rock and Roll," and declares, "Rock and Roll is a river of music that has absorbed many streams: rhythm and blues, jazz, rag time, cowboy songs, country songs, folk songs. All have contributed to the Big Beat."

1954 — Elvis Presley releases the extremely popular single "That's All Right (Mama)."

1955 — "Rock Around the Clock" by Bill Haley & His Comets is released; it tops the U.S. charts and becomes wildly popular in Britain, Australia, and Germany.

1957 — Bill Haley tours Europe.

1957 — Jerry Lee Lewis and Buddy Holly become the first rock musicians to tour Australia.

1960s

1961 — The first Grammy for Best Rock 'n' Roll Recording is awarded to Chubby Checker for *Let's Twist Again*.

1964 — The Beatles make their first visit to America, setting off the British Invasion.

1965 — The psychedelic rock band, the Grateful Dead, is formed in San Francisco.

1967 — The Monterey Pop Festival in California kicks off open air rock concerts.

1969 — The Woodstock Music and Arts Festival attracts a huge crowd to rural upstate New York.

1969 — *Tommy*, the first rock opera, is released by British rock band The Who.

1969 — A rock concert held at Altamont Speedway in California is marred by violence.

1969 — The Rolling Stones tour America as "The Greatest Rock and Roll Band in the World."

1970s

1970 — The Beatles break up.

1971 — Jim Morrison, lead singer of The Doors, dies in Paris.

1971 — Duane Allman, lead guitarist of the Allman Brothers Band, dies.

1973 — *Rolling Stone* magazine names Annie Leibovitz chief photographer and "rock 'n' roll photographer;" she follows and photographs rockers Mick Jagger, John Lennon, and others.

1974 — *Sheer Heart Attack* by the British rock band Queen becomes an international success.

1974 — "Sweet Home Alabama" by Southern rock band Lynyrd Skynyrd is released and becomes an American anthem.

1970s

1975 — *Tommy*, the movie, is released.

1975 — *Time* magazine features Bruce Springsteen on its cover as "Rock's New Sensation."

1979 — Pink Floyd's *The Wall* is released.

1979 — The first Grammy for Best Rock Vocal Performance by a Duo or Group is awarded to The Eagles.

1980s

1980 — John Lennon of the Beatles is murdered in New York City.

1981 — MTV goes on the air.

1981 — *For Those About to Rock We Salute You* by Australian rock band AC/DC becomes the first hard rock album to reach #1 in the U.S.

1985 — Rock stars perform at Live Aid, a benefit concert to raise money to fight Ethiopian famine.

1986 — The Rolling Stones receive a Grammy Lifetime Achievement Award.

1986 — The first Rock and Roll Hall of Fame induction ceremony is held; Chuck Berry, Little Richard, Ray Charles, Elvis Presley, and James Brown, are among the first inductees.

1987 — Billy Joel becomes the first American rock star to perform in the Soviet Union since the construction of the Berlin Wall.

1990s

1991 — Freddie Mercury, lead vocalist of the British rock group Queen, dies of AIDS.

1995 — The Rock and Roll Hall of Fame and Museum opens in Cleveland, Ohio.

2000s

2000s — Aerosmith's album sales reach 140 million worldwide and the group becomes the bestselling American hard rock band of all time.

2003 — Led Zeppelin's "Stairway to Heaven" is inducted into the Grammy Hall of Fame.

2004 — Elton John receives a Kennedy Center Honor.

2004 — *Rolling Stone Magazine* ranks The Beatles #1 of the 100 Greatest Artists of All Time, and Bob Dylan #2.

2005 — Led Zeppelin is ranked #1 on VH1's list of the 100 Greatest Artists of Hard Rock.

2005 — Many rock groups participate in Live 8, a series of concerts to raise awareness of extreme poverty in Africa.

2006 — U2 wins five more Grammys, for a total of 22—the most of any rock artist or group.

2006 — Bob Dylan, at age 65, releases *Modern Times* which immediately rises to #1 in the U.S.

2007 — Billy Joel become the first person to sing the National Anthem before two Super Bowls.

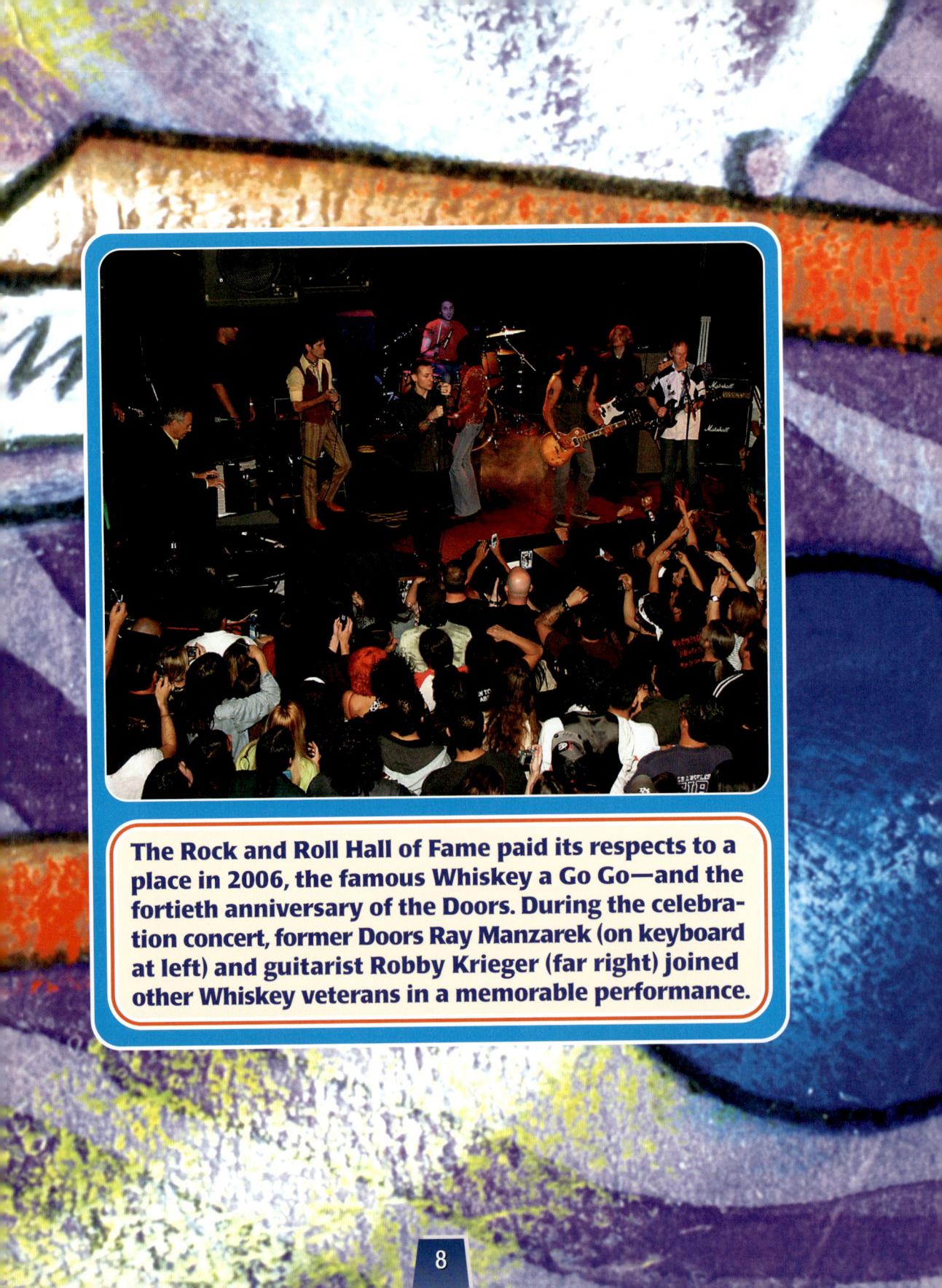

The Rock and Roll Hall of Fame paid its respects to a place in 2006, the famous Whiskey a Go Go—and the fortieth anniversary of the Doors. During the celebration concert, former Doors Ray Manzarek (on keyboard at left) and guitarist Robby Krieger (far right) joined other Whiskey veterans in a memorable performance.

1

Blast from the Past

November 8, 2006, at the Whisky a Go Go club, the rock 'n' roll landmark on Hollywood's famous Sunset Strip, was a big night. Members of a band called the Doors—Ray Manzarek and Robby Krieger— were performing, along with Chester Barrington, of Linkin Park, and Slash, formerly of Guns N'Roses. But the former Doors members were the ones who were really celebrating.

They had good reason to celebrate. After all, 2006 was the fortieth anniversary of their band. And they had gotten their start right there, at the Whisky a Go Go, where they had once played as the house band, way back in the earliest days of their life together.

Whisky a Go Go

The Doors weren't the only famous band that had played at the club during its heyday in the sixties. The Byrds and Buffalo Springfield were regulars at one time. Go-go dancers in cages first performed at the Whisky, and the club stood at the forefront of many musical trends. What's more, it had played an important role in many musical careers besides the Doors', especially for bands based in Southern California. Frank Zappa's Mothers of Invention, for instance, got its first record contract based on a performance at the Whisky. Jimi Hendrix was there to jam when Sam & Dave headlined. In 1966, Otis Redding recorded his album *In Person at the Whisky a Go Go* at the club. The Turtles also played there, and many British performers made their first American performances at the Whisky, including the Kinks, The Who, Cream, Oasis, and Led Zeppelin. The club even made an appearance on film; in *The Graduate*, Dustin Hoffman's character can be seen running out of the Whisky.

In the seventies, the Whisky was at the center of the New Wave and punk movements. The Runaways, X, Mötley Crüe, and Van Halen all played there, and so did the Ramones, the Misfits, Blondie, Talking Heads, Elvis Costello, XTC, and the Jam. But by the 1980s, the Whisky was no longer at the forefront of the music scene. It closed its doors temporarily in the 1982, then reopened in 1986 as a **venue** that could be rented by promoters and bands. Guns N' Roses and Metallica were two of the metal bands that performed there during that era. In the nineties, the Whisky hosted a series of Seattle-based musicians who would later be known as the "godfathers of grunge": Soundgarden, Nirvana, Mudhoney, and the Melvins, among others. In February 2007, the Whisky was still playing its role at the center of rock history when the Police reunited and held a live webcast of their rehearsal at the Whisky.

But for the former members of the Doors on that November night in 2006, the Whisky was a symbol of their past—and their future.

The Doors in the Twenty-First Century

You might think the Doors would seem like some old relic from the past, like a tie-dyed T-shirt that's been washed too many times. But that's far from the case. Although this band was definitely a child of the sixties, with its roots deep in the psychedelic, drug-soaked soil of the decade, like the Whisky, the Doors have managed to make the transition into the twenty-first century.

Blast from the Past

Those gathered to celebrate the Doors' fortieth anniversary and the designation of Whiskey a Go Go as a Rock and Roll Landmark were treated to more than just music. Poetry readings and a book signing by Ray and Robby were also part of the celebration. It was truly a "blast from the past."

On the Doors' Web site, Ray Manzarek talks about the modern relevance of the group:

> "'The Doors are absolutely and completely relevant today because we represent freedom,' says Manzarek, who points out that many alternative rock stars seem to emulate Morrison's look, and that the hip-hop community has been attracted to the Doors'

THE DOORS

Another celebration of the fortieth anniversary of the Doors took place at Book Soup. This time, the group's former drummer, John Densmore (left), paid tribute through music and poetry to Jim Morrison, the band's late lead singer. Though Jim died in 1971, he and his music live on in the memories of music fans all over the world.

> anti-authoritarian vibe. 'When you are at that point in your life where you've left childhood but not yet put on the yoke of adulthood, we represent totally liberating artistic, literary and spiritual freedom. We're about opening the doors of perception in the closed-in, locked-up times we live in now.'

Apparently, Ray hit the nail on the head: young adults still seek freedom from the restrictions of the older generation, and for them, the Doors' message is as fresh and strong as ever. But it's not just teenagers who respond to the Doors' music. Many people, from twelve-year-olds to sixty-two-year-olds, hear the voice at the heart of the Doors' music.

Celebration

Ultimately, that voice belonged to the late Jim Morrison. You'd think that Doors' music would be filled with gloom and hopelessness for those of us who look back on what it all meant within the context of Jim Morrison's tragic life. But again, that's not the case.

On their fortieth anniversary, the surviving members of the Doors wanted to celebrate. They were proud of their past, despite the tragedy, and they were hopeful for the future. And they felt their music still had something important to offer the world of the twenty-first century, a war-torn world that wasn't so very different after all from the sixties' world.

Ray Manzarek said on the Doors' Web site:

> "The ultimate way to spread peace and joy is one person, by one person, by one person, and that's what we're trying to do for our 40th anniversary celebration."

That night at the Whisky, the Doors spread their message of joy. But the music had begun forty years earlier—or actually, forty-one years earlier, on a summer day in 1965.

The birth of the Doors can be traced to a sunny July day in 1965 on a beach in Southern California. Whether by simple chance or the hand of cosmic fate, music-loving college student Ray Manzarek and Jim Morrison first met on that California beach, and a rock legend was born.

2

The Beginning

Do you believe in fate? Or is life built on chance? If you answer the first question with a no, and the second with a yes, then you'd probably say the Doors owe their existence to sheer coincidence. But if you answer yes and then no . . . well, then sooner or later Jim Morrison's and Ray Manzarek's paths were bound to cross.

You see the Doors were born on a July day back in 1965, when two UCLA film students just happened to bump into each other on Venice Beach, California. Jim and Ray were already acquainted with each other, but on that July day, something sparked between them. Jim told Ray that he'd been writing songs. "No kidding?" Ray must have said. "Like what?" And just like that, Jim burst into song.

> "Let's swim to the moon, ah ha,
> Let's climb through the tide,
> Penetrate the evenin' that the
> City sleeps to hide...."

THE DOORS

Ray was so impressed with Jim's lyrics for "Moonlight Drive" that he immediately suggested they form a band together.

Ray, who played the Vox-organ, was already in a band with his brother Rick; they called themselves Rick and the Ravens. Ray also knew a couple of guys from his yoga class who were in rock band; Robby Krieger and John Densmore played in a group called the Psychedelic Rangers. By August, the four guys were playing together; by September, they and the other members of the Ravens, along with a female bass player, had recorded a six-song demo.

What's in a Name?

The group was now complete. All they needed was a name. Rock band names came from everywhere and everything, but the guys wanted a name that meant something to them. They were into expanding their minds through Eastern meditation techniques. On top of that, this was the sixties, after all: like lots of other young people, Jim, Ray, Robby, and John were intrigued with the idea of expanding their minds with drugs.

In 1954, author Aldous Huxley had written a book called *The Doors of Perception*. The title came from a line by the eighteenth-century poet William Blake:

> "If the doors of perception were cleansed every thing would appear to man as it is, infinite. For man has closed himself up, till he sees all things through narrow chinks of his cavern."

Huxley's book describes his experiences while taking **mescaline**. He believed that **psychedelic** drugs had the power to disable the filters that block ultimate reality's messages from reaching the conscious mind. In other words, these drugs, according to Huxley, could open these "doors of perception," allowing people a fuller and more complete awareness of reality.

Jim had ready Huxley many times, and he could quote from memory long passages of his books. "The Doors" seemed the perfect name for the direction Jim and the other guys wanted their band to take. According to Jim:

The Beginning

Even as a young college student, Jim's mind was filled with song lyrics. They seemed to flow from him with ease, sometimes with the slightest of prompts. That's one of the things that led Ray to suggest that he and Jim form a group. Just one month from their first meeting, Ray and Jim had put together the Doors.

THE DOORS

> "There are things known and there are things unknown, and in between are the Doors."

Psychedelic rock music, the kind of music they wanted to make, was intended to reproduce some of the sensations and thoughts that went along with using drugs like LSD. It was music that intended to "open the doors of perception."

From the group's earliest days, it was clear that the Doors weren't like other rock groups. For one thing, the group bucked the trend of using a bass player. Bass guitar played a major role in much of rock music, but Ray generally took care of bass lines by using multiple keyboards.

Jim said of his music:

> "I like any reaction I can get with my music. Just anything to get people to think. I mean if you can get a whole room full of drunk, stoned people to actually wake up and think, you're doing something."

Technique and Talent

Philosophy aside, the guys were serious about making music. Unlike other rock groups, however, they did not normally use a bass guitarist. Instead, Ray played the bass lines with his left hand on the newly invented Fender Rhodes bass keyboard, while he used his right hand to play other keyboards. In the recording studio, the group occasionally did use bass players, including Jerry Scheff, Doug Lubahn, Harvey Brooks, Kerry Magness, Lonnie Mack, Leroy Vinegar, and Ray Neapolitan.

The entire group helped compose the songs. Jim and Robbie usually came up with the basic lyrics and melody, but the others contributed their ideas for harmony and rhythm. For example, the long organ introduction at the beginning of "Light My Fire" was Ray's idea.

Fired! Signed!

By the following year, the group was going strong. They went from playing at the London Fog Club to the more **prestigious** club called Whisky a Go Go. Jac Holzman, the president of Elektra Records, and producer Paul Rothchild came into the club on August 10, 1966, and heard the Doors play. They liked what they heard. They liked it a lot.

Just a few weeks later, however, Jim got in trouble at the club. On the night of August 21, Jim was tripping on something; under the influence of whatever chemical he was using, he created his own version of *Oedipus Rex*, the famous Greek tragedy, in which the hero unknowingly kills his father and has sex with his mother. Jim's rendition of these events was so crude—and used so many four-letter words—that the club's owner fired him on the spot.

But the Doors didn't care as much as they might have. Because as things turned out, they didn't really need Whisky a Go Go anymore. Elektra Records had just signed a contract with them. Their real career was ready to take off.

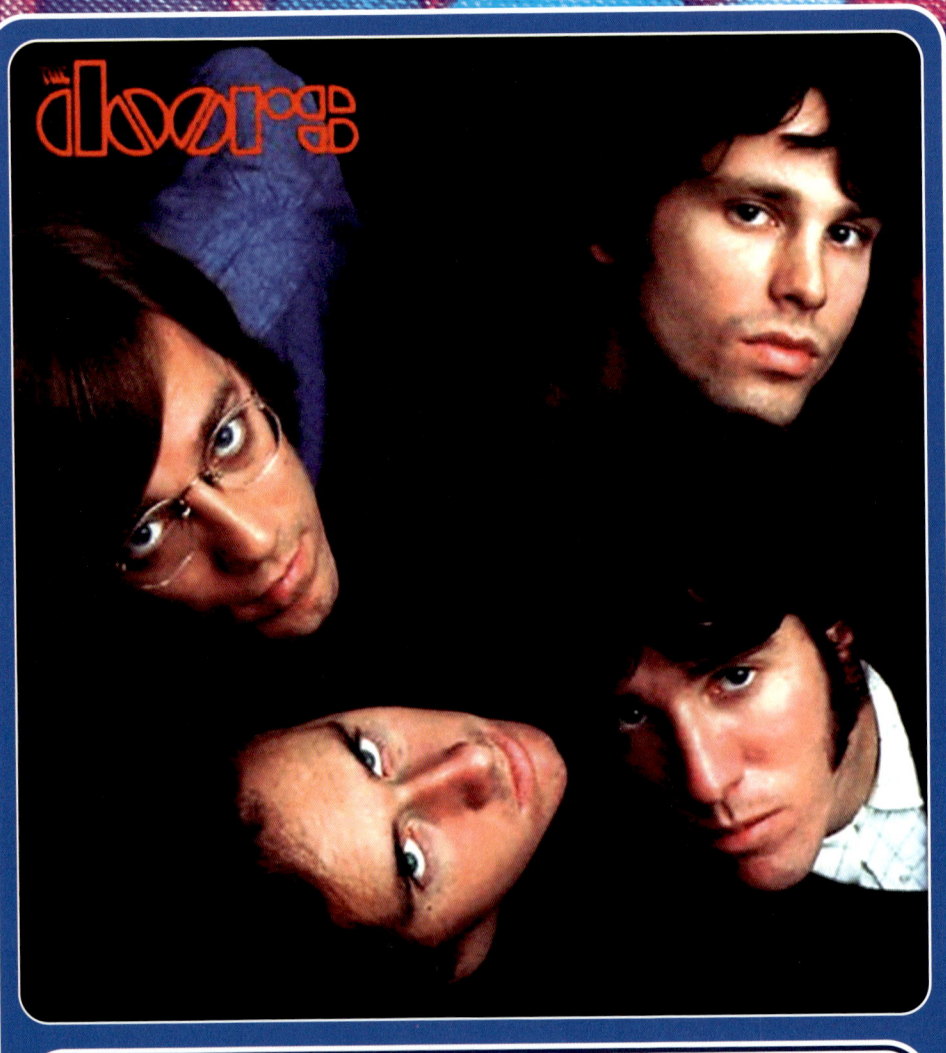

Before long, the Doors had a recording contract with Elektra. John, Ray, Robby, and Jim were on their way to rock legend status. Fans and critics were intrigued by the band and its lead vocalist. But it was not just the music that would bring the group fame and legendary status.

3

Finding Fame

In August 1966, after the Doors had been together a year, they recorded their first album with Elektra Records, *The Doors*. It featured most of their major songs, including the eleven-minute musical drama, "The End." The entire album was recorded in the space of a few days, almost entirely live in the studio.

Success!

The album featured "Alabama Song," originally written by Bertolt Brecht and Kurt Weill for the opera *Aufstieg und Fall der Stadt Mahagonny*. The Doors also included "Back Door Man," a **cover** of a song by the blues legend Howlin' Wolf. In addition to the music, Jim and Ray created something no one else had ever done before: a promotional film for a single. The film for their "Break on Through" became an early forerunner of today's music videos. When the album was released, it caused a major sensation in music circles. Critics were impressed—and the Doors earned themselves a whole new circle of fans.

The second single from the album, "Light My Fire," was released in April 1967. It immediately propelled the Doors into fame, putting them alongside Jefferson Airplane and the Grateful Dead as one of America's top psychedelic rock bands.

Rebels

As their success gained steam, the Doors picked up a reputation for being outrageous and rebellious. Jim, with his sexy good looks, his spellbinding stage presence, and his trademark skin-tight leather pants, was the one who stirred up the most feelings, both good and bad. Jim seemed to have a knack for getting people to pay attention to him—and he was self-aware enough to know what he was doing. He said:

> "I think that more than writing and music, my greatest talent is that I have an instinctive knack of self-image propagation. I was very good at manipulating publicity with a few little phrases [that got people upset]. Having grown up with TV and mass magazines, I knew instinctively what people would catch on to, so I dropped those little jewels here and there, seemingly very innocently; of course, I was just calling signals."

But while Jim liked the attention, he didn't like all the expectations that came along with being famous. He wanted the freedom to be himself, no matter how much that might upset other people. He said:

> "We're like actors, turned loose in this world to wander in search of a phantom, endlessly searching for a half-formed shadow of our lost reality. When others demand that we become the people they want us to be, they force us to destroy the person we really are. It's a subtle kind of murder."

Jim did not give in easily to the pressure to be what others wanted. This became all too clear on September 17, 1967, when the Doors made their first appearance on national television, on *The Ed Sullivan Show*.

Finding Fame 23

There was no fighting it: Jim Morrison had that "something" that drew people to him, including a legion of fiercely loyal fans. Onstage he was sexy, spellbinding, and certainly knew how to sell himself to the audience. But his outrageousness and rebelliousness didn't end when Jim stepped off stage.

Getting on this show was pretty much a requirement in the sixties for anyone hoping to achieve fame and fortune in the world of entertainment, so the Doors' invitation from Mr. Sullivan was an achievement in itself. However, the CBS network censors weren't happy with some of the Doors' lyrics. They insisted that the line in "Light My Fire," "Girl, we couldn't get much higher," be changed to "Girl, we couldn't get much better," to avoid any possible reference to drug use. The band members agreed—but when Jim sang the song live on the air, he sang the original line.

There was nothing CBS could do. Ed Sullivan was furious and refused to shake hands with the band members at the end of the show. Jim insisted that he hadn't meant to sing the original line, that he'd been nervous and had sung the line out of habit, without thinking. CBS and Ed Sullivan didn't care. They told the band members they would never be invited back to the program again.

Jim and the other guys didn't really care. After all, they'd already been on the show, and that was all they needed to cement their place in rock 'n' roll fame. And Jim had no intention of "playing the game" in the future, either. He was more interested in exploring the dark side of himself, the side of himself that was full of unacceptable forces and wild urges. He said:

> "I think there's a whole region of images and feelings inside us that rarely are given outlet in daily life. And when they do come out, they can take **perverse** forms. It's the dark side. Everyone, when he sees it, recognizes the same thing in himself. It's a recognition of forces that rarely see the light of day. The more civilized we get on the surface, the more the other forces make their plea."

Jim seemed determined to give those dark forces inside him every chance to come out. A few months later, on December 10, he badmouthed the local police during a concert at New Haven, Connecticut. The police had apparently caught him earlier backstage with a girl, and they had gone so far as to use Mace on the rock star. When Jim told the audience what had happened, the police were not amused; they arrested Jim.

Jim's rebellious antics were an important part of how he viewed both the world and himself. He felt his behavior was more than just a statement against the powers-that-be; it was inspirational, even spiritual. He said:

> "I am interested in anything about revolt, disorder, chaos—especially activity that seems to have no

Finding Fame

> meaning. It seems to me to be the road toward freedom.... Rather than starting inside, I start outside and reach the mental through the physical."

A Very Good Year

Despite Jim's antics (or maybe because of them), 1967 was a very good year for the Doors. They finished out the year by recording "Light My Fire" and "Moonlight Drive" live for the *Jonathan Winters Show*, and

In 1967, the police were onstage with the Doors. They were performing all right, but not musically; they were performing their law enforcement duties. The police had caught Jim misbehaving backstage before the concert. Jim didn't like the way they treated him, so when he took the stage at the Connecticut concert, he badmouthed the officers. He was arrested.

then from December 26 through 28, they played at the Winterland Ballroom in San Francisco. Author Stephen Davis, in his biography of Jim, described a scene from their performance:

> **"The next night at Winterland, a TV set was wheeled onstage during the Doors' set so the band could see themselves on the *Jonathan Winters Show*. They stopped playing "Back Door Man" when their song came on (there were no home VCRs as yet). The audience watched the Doors watching themselves on TV."**

The Doors played two more concerts in 1967, this time in Denver on December 30 and 31, finishing off a year of almost constant touring.

Strange Days

The Doors' second album, *Strange Days*, was less spontaneous and more carefully produced than their first one had been. Despite this, Jim's lyrics and the near-**mystical** atmosphere they created combined with the music and established Jim's reputation as a spiritual but sexy magician-priest. The album included such now-classic songs as "People Are Strange" and "Love Me Two Times."

After the success of the Doors' second album, some of their fans felt the group had sold out to **commercialism**. Band members had allowed *Sixteen* magazine to portray them as teen idols, and around the same time, people began to wise up to the fact that the band's "spontaneous" wildness at their concerts was actually planned out ahead of time. In February 1968, *Rolling Stone* expressed its new **cynicism** about the Doors' performances:

> **"One shtick, or piece of stage-business, missing at the Shrine performance, was Morrison's carefully-executed 'accidental' fall from the stage into the crowd. For months this had been a part of the act. It got a lot of screams from the teenyboppers. Then a review appeared in a local newspaper which called the fall one of the phoniest things ever. Morrison was asked if he had read the article. 'Yeah,' said**

Finding Fame

> Morrison, 'and I guess he's right.' Morrison did not take the fall that night at the Shrine."

A new tension seemed to be hanging around the Doors. In May 1968, they played a series of outdoor shows, including at the Chicago Coliseum, where their fans grew so frenzied that the police were called in to calm things down. Meanwhile, Jim was becoming increasingly dependent on alcohol.

Fans never knew what to expect during a Doors concert, especially from Jim. For a while, he would seem to accidentally fall from the stage and into the adoring crowd. Other times Jim fell to the stage and appeared to be unconscious. Jim Morrison certainly knew the definition of showmanship.

THE DOORS

Later, Jim said:

"People are afraid of themselves, of their own reality; their feelings most of all. People talk about how great love is, but . . . love hurts. Feelings are disturbing. People are taught that pain is evil and dangerous. How can they deal with love if they're afraid to feel? Pain is meant to wake us up. People try to hide their pain. But they're wrong. Pain is something to carry, like a radio. You feel your strength in the experience of

Waiting for the Sun was the group's first album to hit #1 on the charts. In this photo, the guys are shown receiving recognition for the album's success from executives of Elektra Records. Not everyone was happy with the album, including some of the group's fans. Some felt the group had forgotten what had first made them a success.

> pain. It's all in how you carry it. That's what matters. Pain is a feeling. Your feelings are a part of you. Your own reality. If you feel ashamed of them, and hide them, you're letting society destroy your reality. You should stand up for your right to feel your pain."

But despite these wise words, Jim spent much of his life struggling with his pain and his own reality. And at this point in his life, he turned to alcohol to help him deaden the pain of being himself.

Waiting for the Sun

That same spring the Doors launched immediately into recording their third album. By now they had recorded all their original songs; it was time to create new material. Despite the clouds that were beginning to gather, their new work proved to both their fans and the critics that the Doors' talent was undiminished.

Waiting for the Sun was the Doors' first #1 album; the single from the album, "Hello, I Love You," became their second (and last) #1 single in the United States. The album also included the song "The Unknown Soldier," and the band created another self-directed movie video to bring this song to life. Jim and the others had created a thirty-minute work called "Celebration of the Lizard" that was far too long to include on the album, but they excerpted a shorter song from it, "Not to Touch the Earth."

Despite the success and creativity of this new work, however, some of the Doors' original fans were disappointed yet again. With their latest successes, the band had now completely left behind their **underground**, counterculture roots. Author Lilian Roxon wrote in *Rock Encyclopedia*:

> "As triumph piled on triumph for the Doors—packed auditoriums, television appearances, riots, hit after hit, albums in the top hundred, fees soaring and soaring—the underground drew back, first in dismay, then in disgust. Incredible, incredible, the Doors, of all people, had sold out. . . . And the third album, *Waiting for the Sun*, strengthened the dreadful suspicion that the Doors were in it just for the money."

THE DOORS

The Doors went to Britain and Europe in 1968. Though the near-riot conditions that had plagued many of the group's U.S. stops didn't occur on this tour, Jim's self-destructive behavior did. When he collapsed on an Amsterdam stage during a concert, this time it was no publicity stunt; it was the real thing, brought on by drug abuse.

Adding to the Doors' fans' sense of disillusionment was the fact that one of the songs on *Waiting for the Sun*, "Hello, I Love You," sounded a whole lot like a Kinks' song. The band members insisted it wasn't intentional, but many people felt the songs were simply too similar. What had happened to the Doors' originality and creativity? What was going on?

Crash

Meanwhile, the Doors concerts kept turning into riots that called for police intervention. Jim's antics seemed out of control. And the publicity just kept churning.

The group flew to Britain for their first concerts outside North America. In London, they held a press conference at the ICA Gallery, and then they played a series of shows at the Roundhouse Theatre. The concerts were broadcast on a Granada TV show called "The Doors Are Open" (which was later released as a video). The band then went on to play across Europe.

And then in Amsterdam, everything crashed. Jim collapsed after a drug binge. He returned to London in September 1968, and he stayed there a month, recovering. Clearly, Jim was not coping with fame. He had set out to open doors in people's minds—but instead, he found himself playing a role that he couldn't keep up with.

He said:

> "Most people love you for who you pretend to be. To keep their love, you keep pretending—performing. You get to love your pretence. It's true, we're locked in an image, an act—and the sad thing is, people get so used to their image, they grow attached to their masks. They love their chains. They forget all about who they really are."

Jim's insights seem based on his own life. He was pretending, performing for all he was worth; he'd grown attached to the superstar mask he wore; and addiction was becoming another set of chains. Apparently, Jim had forgotten who he really was.

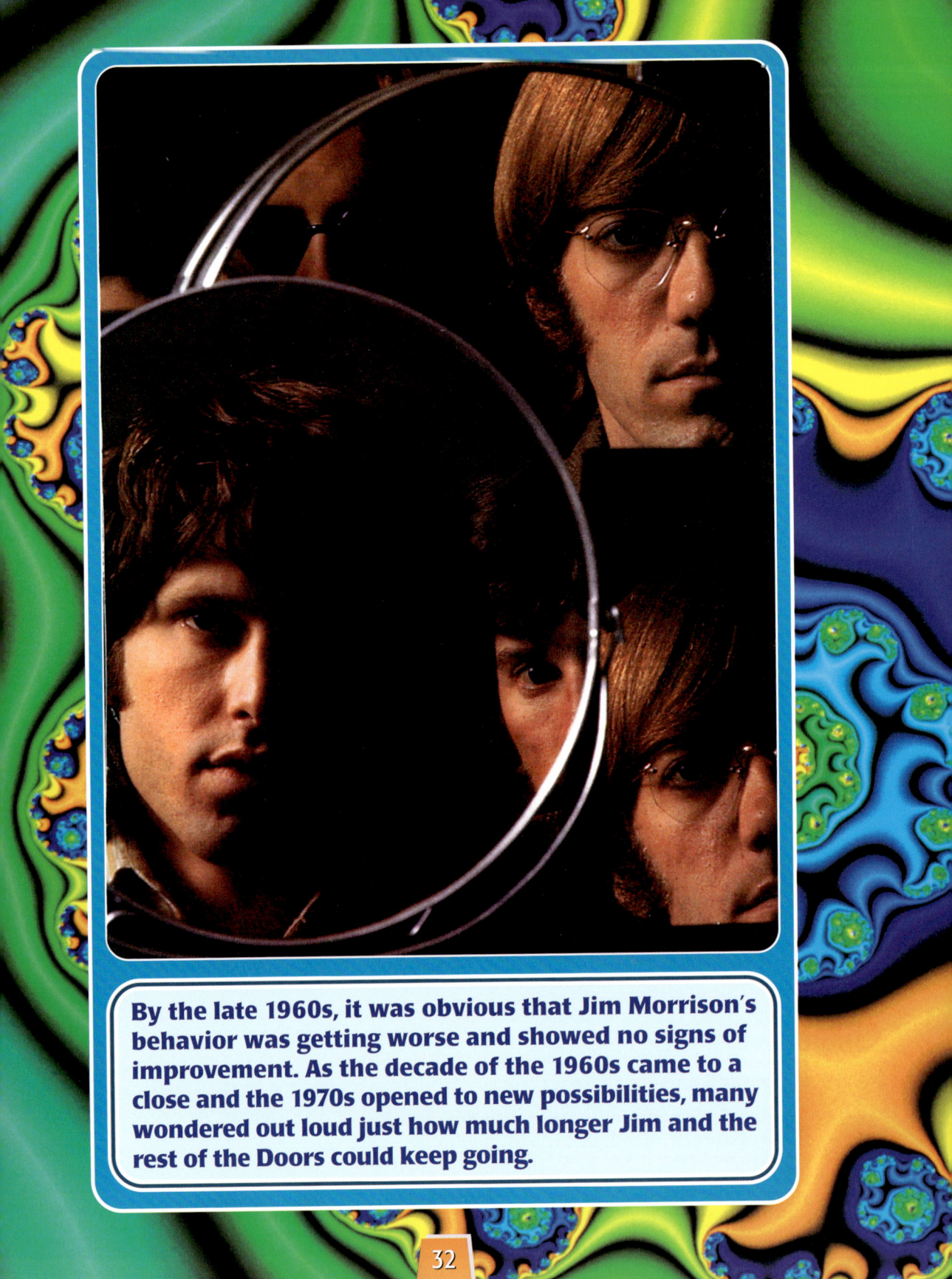

By the late 1960s, it was obvious that Jim Morrison's behavior was getting worse and showed no signs of improvement. As the decade of the 1960s came to a close and the 1970s opened to new possibilities, many wondered out loud just how much longer Jim and the rest of the Doors could keep going.

Drugs, Destruction, and Death

Despite Jim's troubles, the group kept going through the rest of 1968. In November of that year, they began work on their fourth album. They played nine more U.S. concerts, and things seemed back on track, at least for the time being. But 1969 would be a difficult year for them.

The year started out a high note, though, with a sold-out show in January at New York City's famous Madison Square Garden, followed by a successful new single, "Touch Me," which made it to #3 on the U.S. charts.

Freedom?

The next month, in February 1969, Jim attended a theater production at the University of Southern California that had a powerful influence on both him and the other members of the band. The Living Theatre presented a **controversial** show that urged people to become free by casting aside all their **inhibitions**.

Freedom was an important concept for Jim, one with which he constantly struggled. He said:

> **"The most important kind of freedom is to be what you really are. You trade in your reality for a role. You trade in your sense for an act. You give up your ability to feel, and in exchange, put on a mask."**

Jim took to heart the theater production's message. The following evening, he and the other band members had a famous jam session, which became known as "Rock Is Dead." (It was later released in 1997 in the Doors box set.) This session of frenzied, uninhibited music set the stage for the events that followed.

On March 1, 1969, the Doors were scheduled to perform at the Dinner Key Auditorium in Miami, Florida. Jim missed his original flight to the show, and he killed time by drinking. Meanwhile, the concert had been oversold by almost double the hall's capacity, and fans were piled up in a sweltering auditorium with no air conditioning. By the time the band finally walked on stage, people were desperate—and Jim was drunk as a skunk.

Jim bellowed into the microphone, encouraging the angry audience—and society in general—to "lighten up," as the Living Theatre people had advised. He then rambled on for several minutes, not making much sense at all, and finally concluded by shouting, "Anything you want! Let's do it! Let's do it! Let's do it!" At that point, the story goes, he exposed himself to the audience.

Afterward, Jim faced legal charges of indecent exposure, and the incident damaged the band's reputation. Jim for one didn't seem to mind. His outrageous behavior was a little like a child's whose acting out is actually a cry for help. In this case, Jim certainly used inappropriate means to get what he wanted—but he did achieve the goal for which he secretly longed: time off from the enormous pressure of being a rock star. Concerts were cancelled, and suddenly, Jim had time again to write poetry. He said later:

Drugs, Destruction, and Death

> **"I think I was just fed up with the image that had been created around me . . . and so I put an end to it in one glorious evening."**

In April 1969, Jim began shooting footage for *HWY*, an experimental film about a hitchhiker, played by Jim himself. The film, which contains almost no dialogue at all, was never officially released, but it circulated among Doors collectors.

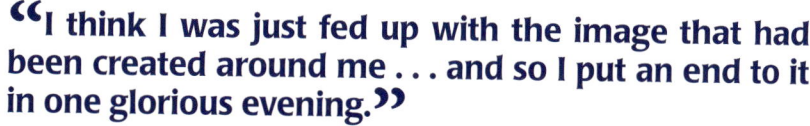

Sometimes it seemed as though Jim was in the spotlight more for his misbehaviors than for his music. During a 1969 Miami concert, a drunk Jim allegedly exposed himself to a crowd who had grown increasingly impatient waiting for the group to perform. Here, Jim and his attorney are shown during one of their trips to court.

THE DOORS

Jim's "Family"

Through all the turmoil, the band remained loyal to Jim—and he depended on them to get him through many of the challenges in his life. He had never been close to his birth family, but now, the other band members filled that role in his life.

Jim clearly received more attention than the other band members. It was his face that appeared on album covers, and he was the troubled

Through all of Jim's difficulties, there was one thing he could be sure of: Ray, Robby, and John would stand by him. Not once did they waiver in their support of their troubled lead singer. They were more than a group; they were a family, and a family doesn't give up on one of their own—no matter what.

Drugs, Destruction, and Death

sex idol that attracted the adoration of female fans. But before one concert, when the announcer introduced the band as "Jim Morrison and the Doors," Jim refused to come on stage until the announcer changed the introduction to merely "the Doors." Solo opportunities also came Jim's way, but he turned them all down.

Surprisingly, despite the outrageous ways he hammed it up on stage, Jim was shy in social situations. He told Ray once that he never felt comfortable around people unless Ray or another member of the band was there with him.

Trouble

Jim cut back on his drug use—but he kept on drinking. He drank so much that he gained weight, losing his "Lizard King" look; he was no longer lean and sexy in leather.

By June, the Doors were back on tour, hitting the Chicago Auditorium Theater, and then the Aquarius Theatre in Hollywood the following month. These concerts were different from early Doors performances. No longer was there the expectation that each concert would be a mystical experience intended to open the doors of the audience's souls. Instead, the emphasis was on the band and their fans simply having a good time together. Jim, now wearing a beard, no longer slunk across the stage in tight leather, and he was setting a bluesier tone for the band with songs like "I Will Never Be Untrue," "Who Do You Love?" and "Build Me a Woman." His critics and his fans agreed, though: Jim's voice was as powerful as ever.

When the Doors' fourth album, *The Soft Parade,* was released that same month, however, their old underground fans felt completely abandoned. The new album contained songs that were very "pop," including horn sections that sounded like something out of Vegas. (The single "Touch Me" featured saxophonist Curtis Amy.) The album sold—but it had lost the spiritual overtones that had once been so important to Jim and the others.

During the album's production, Jim's ongoing drinking had made it hard for him to keep to any sort of recording schedule, plus he was moody and difficult. The Doors had once been famous for how quickly they could lay down tracks, but the album's recording sessions had dragged on for weeks. Studio costs mounted as a result. Critics said all these difficulties showed in the final product. The Doors were struggling just to keep going, claimed the critics, and the result was an overproduced album that tried to use horns and strings to disguise its basic weakness. Other critics, however, spoke up on behalf of the album. They said the Doors' talent came through loud and clear in the lyrics and guitar work.

Recording their next album the following November didn't go much better. And Jim was still drinking and still getting into trouble. On a flight to Phoenix, Arizona (where he planned to attend a Rolling Stones concert), Jim got in trouble with the law again when he became drunk and was abusive to airline attendants. (He was eventually **acquitted** the following April, when an airline steward mistook Jim for his traveling companion, actor Tom Baker.)

1970

The year started on a hopeful note for the Doors. Their fifth album, *Morrison Hotel*, was released early in the year, and many considered it a strong return to the Doors' roots. All the songs had a hard-rock sound, and they rang with a new sense of celebration and hope that had been missing from the band's earlier music. The album hit #4 on the U.S. lists.

The Doors toured all through the summer. In August, they were part of the Isle of Wight Festival along with other music legends, including Jimi Hendrix, Joni Mitchell, Sly & the Family Stone, The Who, and Miles Davis.

Meanwhile, Jim's legal problems had not disappeared. In September, he faced a jury trial for his behavior back in Miami. The jury returned a verdict of guilty of profanity and indecent exposure, and Jim was sentenced to eight months' custody. However, he was allowed to go free, pending an appeal of his case.

At the end of the year, on December 8, Jim celebrated his twenty-seventh birthday by recording more of his poetry. His life was unraveling at the seams—but his talent was undiminished.

The End

The Doors' last public appearance was four days after his birthday at the Warehouse in New Orleans. In the middle of the concert, Jim had some sort of psychiatric break and slammed the microphone over and over onto the stage floor.

Drugs, Destruction, and Death

As the 1970s began, it was a different Jim Morrison who fronted the Doors. As shown on this cover of *The History of Rock*, gone was the clean-shaven, thin, leather-clad rock star. In his place was a heavier, bearded, less provocatively dressed Jim. The group's music also took on a new direction.

THE DOORS

Fans seemed to like the group's new sound (at least Jim's voice), but that didn't mean smooth sailing for the band. Recording sessions sometimes went on much longer than expected, which made the albums more expensive to produce, because of Jim's temperamental behavior. Jim still drank heavily, and he still managed to get in trouble with the police.

And yet, as the new year opened, the Doors had a new album, *L.A. Woman*, that was gathering great reviews. The band had aimed for it to be a back-to-basics work, and many felt that it was their greatest work since their earliest music. The songs, which included "Love Her Madly" and "Riders on the Storm," explored the band's **blues** and **R&B** roots.

Jim knew he was in trouble personally, though, and he decided to take some time off from the band. In March, he moved to Paris with his girlfriend, Pamela Courson, and for a time, he seemed to

Drugs, Destruction, and Death

be getting his act together. He wrote and explored Paris and tried to cut back on his drinking.

By May, however, he was drinking so heavily that he fell out of a second-story window. The following month, as he wandered drunk through the streets of Paris, he bumped into two street musicians and invited them to accompany him to a recording studio. (The results of this session, Jim's last recording, were eventually released in 1994 on a **bootleg** CD titled *The Lost Paris Tapes*.)

Death

Jim had been preoccupied with death for a long time. He seemed to sense that it was looming over him. He said:

> "I wouldn't mind dying in a plane crash. It'd be a good way to go. I don't want to die in my sleep, or of old age, or OD.... I want to feel what it's like. I want to taste it, hear it, smell it. Death is only going to happen to you once; I don't want to miss it."

Jim didn't get his wish; in the end, he missed his own death and left life in a state of unconsciousness.

On July 3, 1971, he was found dead in the bathtub of his apartment. The official verdict was that he had died of a heart attack, but no autopsy was ever conducted. Rumors persisted for years that Jim had merely faked his death to escape the mess his life had become. Others claimed that he had actually died in a Paris nightclub, and his body had later been taken secretly to his apartment. Author Danny Sugerman, in his book *Wonderland Avenue*, tells a different story. In his last interview with Jim's girlfriend, Pamela Courson, she confessed that she had accidentally given Jim an overdose of heroin. Jim was afraid of needles, so she shot him up—and killed him.

A Shooting Star

Jim Morrison never managed to get a lot of things right. From one perspective, you could say his story is one of failure and lack of control. Addiction destroyed him. But that's not the whole story. Despite the problems that eventually led to his death, Jim never gave up hope. His rebellion against the world may have looked to many like

THE DOORS

It's an odd thing, but when someone famous dies under what some might call unusual conditions, there often is a rush to find a conspiracy or other sinister circumstances surrounding the death. That was certainly true when Jim Morrison died in 1971. Author Danny Sugerman put some of the rumors to rest in his book *Wonderland Avenue*.

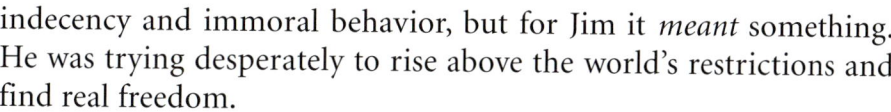

Drugs, Destruction, and Death

indecency and immoral behavior, but for Jim it *meant* something. He was trying desperately to rise above the world's restrictions and find real freedom.

Jim once said:

> "A hero is someone who rebels or seems to rebel against the facts of existence and seems to conquer them. Obviously that can only work at moments. It can't be a lasting thing. That's not saying that people shouldn't keep trying to rebel against the facts of existence. Someday, who knows, we might conquer death, disease and war."

Jim's voice of rebellion still continues. While his life is a warning against following his example too closely, yet he also continues to inspire us to keep seeking real truth, real freedom: to find the way to open the closed doors in our minds and see what we can conquer.

Another time, Jim said of himself:

> "I see myself as a huge fiery comet, a shooting star. Everyone stops, points up and gasps 'Oh look at that!' Then—whoosh, and I'm gone . . . and they'll never see anything like it ever again, and they won't be able to forget me—ever."

Jim was right. No one would ever forget him.

Now what? Jim's death hit the Doors hard. Not only had Ray, Robby, and John (from left) lost their vocalist and primary songwriter, they had lost a friend and family member. Though Jim had always insisted the group was the Doors, not Jim Morrison and the Doors, there was no doubt that he had been the face of the group.

After Jim

Life without Jim would never be the same—but the other band members tried to keep going. They considered finding a new singer to replace him—Iggy Pop was considered—but in the end, Ray and Robbie took over the band's vocals. The Doors released two more albums—*Other Voices* and *Full Circle*—and they went on tour.

The first album was true to the old Doors roots, but the second one expanded into new territory with a much jazzier sound. Both new albums sold well, though not in the numbers they had when Jim was alive. By the end of 1972, however, the band members faced the truth: the Doors were done. They stopped performing and recording; they stopped trying to go on without Jim.

Jim's Legacy

But there was still work out there of Jim's that had never been released, and in 1978, the remaining band members added a musical track to the spoken-word recordings of Jim reading his own poetry. The result, *An American Prayer*, sold enough to make some money for the remaining band members. They followed this up with a mini-album of previously unreleased live material from Jim's days with the band.

The Doors might not be creating new music; they were no longer giving concerts; but that didn't mean they weren't still winning new fans. Doors music continued to be played on FM radio stations throughout the 1970s, the '80s, winning a whole new generation of listeners who loved their sound and related to their message.

In 1979, one of Jim's old friends from the film school at UCLA, Francis Ford Coppola, released the movie *Apocalypse Now*, and he used the Doors song "The End" in the sound track. The movie helped a new batch of fans discover the Doors.

A few years later, in 1983, the Doors released another live album, *Alive, She Cried*, which included a cover of the Them hit, "Gloria."

Then, as the nineties began, film director Oliver Stone focused attention once again on the Doors with the movie *The Doors*. Val Kilmer played Jim, and Robbie and John made cameo appearances in the file. Many critics loved Kilmer's portrayal of Jim, but the film wasn't completely accurate. Members of the Doors were upset that Stone made Jim look like a **sociopath**; they felt the movie had failed to capture the many moral shades of gray that would have made Jim's story more true to reality. As his friends, they felt the movie denied Jim the right to be simply himself.

Friends and Fans Forever

Jim would have been grateful for his friends' loyalty. His relationship with them was apparently one of the best things in his life, a force that helped him hold onto himself when everything else was working to pull him into pieces. He said:

> "Friends can help each other. A true friend is someone who lets you have total freedom to be yourself—and especially to feel. Or, not feel. Whatever you happen to be feeling at the moment is fine with them. That's what real love amounts to—letting a person be what he really is."

After Jim

Famous film director Francis Ford Coppola was one of Jim's college friends. In 1979, Coppola released his tribute to the rock legend, *The Doors*. The film featured Val Kilmer as the troubled Jim Morrison and Meg Ryan as his girlfriend, Pamela Courson. The movie introduced new people to the Doors' music.

But people hadn't understood Jim when he was alive, and many certainly didn't after he was dead. However, although Jim's life may have been just as controversial and shocking to many people as it had ever been, that didn't mean his talent was being overlooked, even after his death.

In 1993, the Doors were **inducted** into the Rock and Roll Hall of Fame. (Other inductees that year included Ruth Brown, Cream, Creedence Clearwater Revival, Frankie Lyman and the Teenagers, Etta James, Van Morrison, and Sly & the Family Stone.) In 1998, *Q* magazine readers voted *Strange Days* #93 of the Greatest Album of All Times.

In November 2000, the remaining members of the Doors announced the creation of Bright Midnight Records, a label that would make available to the public on CD thirty-six albums and ninety hours of previously unreleased Morrison-era Doors material. Bright Midnight Records launched itself with a sampler of forthcoming material, mostly from live concerts. The first full release was a two-CD set of a May 1970 show at Detroit's Cobo Arena; the concert was memorable for being, according to Doors manager Danny Sugerman, "easily . . . the longest Doors' set ever performed." Two CDs of interviews, mostly with Morrison, followed this release; after this, came CDs of the two 1969 shows at the Aquarius and one of the rehearsals. Next came a four-CD set, *Boot Yer But*, that included bootleg-quality material. Doors' fans didn't care; this CD sold out, maybe because it included a song from the Doors' final show in December 1970.

In November 2006, the *Perception* box set was released; it contained the Doors' six studio albums plus about two hours of mostly unheard studio outtakes. Two discs represented each album: a CD of the album and the bonus tracks, and a DVD with mostly previously released video footage. The discs came with new liner notes and articles from music critics and historians for each album. Demand was so high for the *Perception* box set that the company was sold out in three weeks.

The Doors' remaining members knew that their history together—and the music they had made—was still something people would pay money to hear. But Robby and Ray also wanted to create music in the present.

After Jim | 49

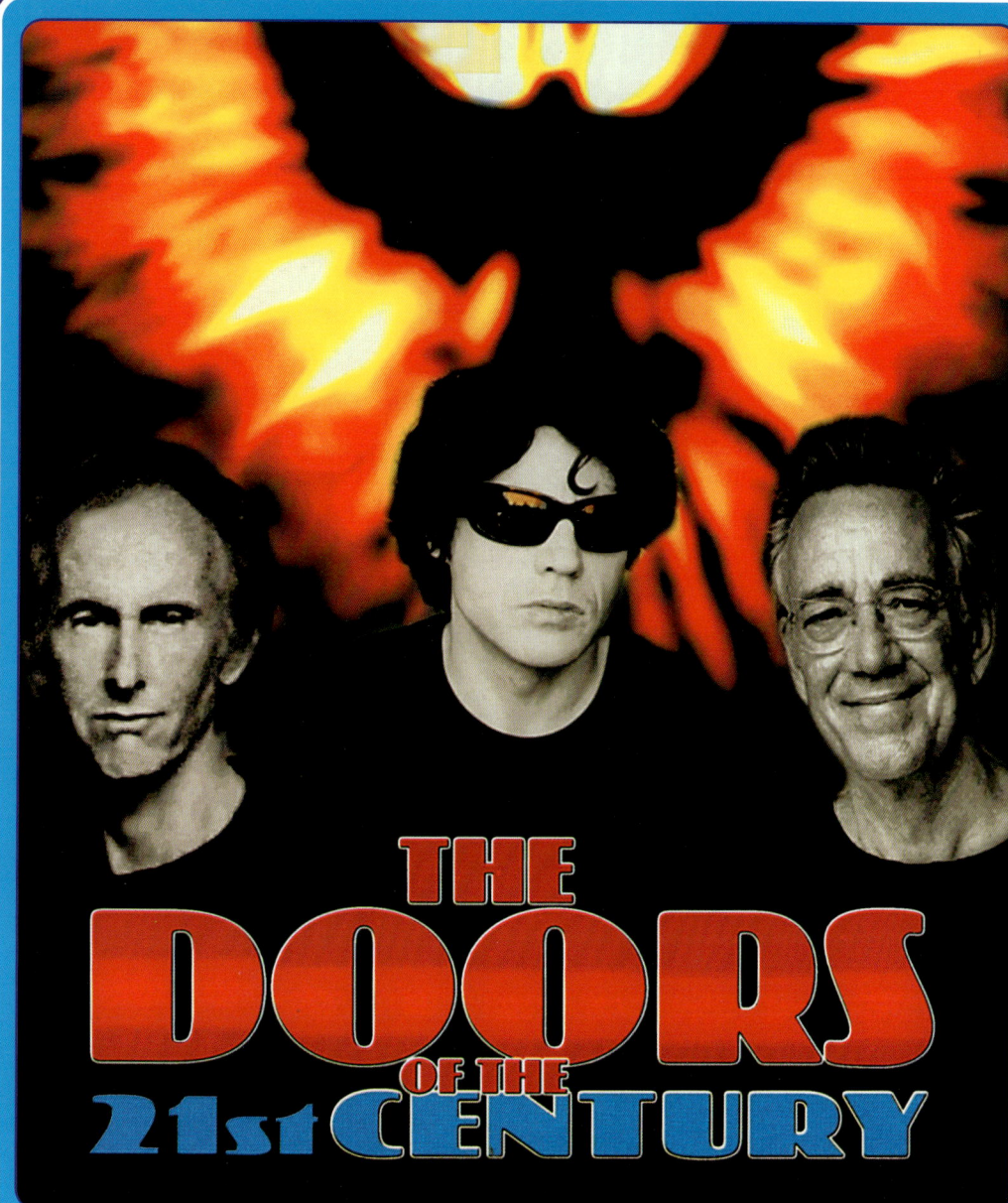

THE DOORS OF THE 21st CENTURY

In 2002, Robby and Ray joined with vocalist Ian Astbury (center) to form the Doors of the 21st Century. John didn't participate: Ray and Robby claim a medical condition made it impossible, but John says no one asked him. Legal battles occurred over the use of the name the Doors, with the Doors of the 21st Century a compromise.

The New Doors

Finally, in 2002 Ray and Robby reunited, creating a new version of the Doors: the Doors of the 21st Century. Ian Astbury was the new frontman, and Angelo Barbera played bass. At their first concert, the group revealed that John would not be able to perform with them as their drummer, because he now suffered from tinnitus (a condition where the sufferer seems to hear constant noise from within his ear). John was initially replaced with Stewart Copeland from the Police, but this did not work out. (Copeland broke his arm in a bicycle accident, and the relationship disintegrated into lawsuits.) Eventually, Ty Dennis took over as the new drummer.

Later, however, John claimed that he had never even been invited to take part in the reunion. In February 2003, he filed an injunction against his former bandmates, trying to prevent them from using the name "Doors." His motion was denied in court. Ray made a public invitation to John, asking him to be a part of the new group, but apparently, the bad feelings were not so easily healed.

Meanwhile, Jim's family and the family of his girlfriend, Pamela Courson (who died from a heroin overdose in 1974), joined with John in his legal battle to keep the "new Doors" from using the name. In July 2005, John and Jim's estate were victorious, and the band changed its name to D21C. It now plays under the name Riders on the Storm. It can also use names such as "former Doors" or "members of the Doors."

Disagreements

John has also made sure that the band never licenses Doors music for use in television commercials, despite a $15 million offer from Cadillac to lease the song "Break on Through (to the Other Side)." According to John, to use Doors music to sell a product would be against everything the Doors once stood for. He wrote in *The Nation*:

> "I've had people say kids died in Vietnam listening to this music, other people say they know someone who didn't commit suicide because of this music.... On stage, when we played these songs, they felt mysterious and magic. That's not for rent."

After Jim

John (shown here holding a copy of *The Doors by the Doors*) has gone to great lengths to fight commercial use of the Doors' music. He believes that to use the group's music to sell products would be against everything Jim and the band had stood for. Ray and Robby claim that doing so would help the band live on.

THE DOORS

The Doors are still being recognized for their accomplishments. The Grammy Foundation gave the group a Lifetime Achievement Award in 2007. Also in 2007, the band received a star on the famous Hollywood Walk of Fame in Los Angeles. Robby (left) and Ray (right) were on hand for the ceremony.

But Ray and Robby disagree. They believe that licensing Doors music to advertisers would be a way to keep the music alive, to keep the Doors from fading into history. According to Ray, that's what Jim would have wanted. Ray said in *Word* magazine:

> "We're all getting older. We should, the three of us, be playing these songs because, hey, the end is always near. Morrison was a poet, and above all, a poet wants his words heard. In fact, on several occasions, when asked what he would most like to be remembered for, Morrison responded, 'My words, man, my words.'"

Doors Forever

If John has his way, Doors music will never become a part of our cultural consciousness through commercials. And yet Jim Morrison and the Doors are still very much a part of rock 'n' roll history. Tribute bands play their songs—and their music continues to sell.

In 2002, *Strange Days* placed at #42 on *Rolling Stone*'s 500 Greatest Albums of All Time. The following year, in 2003, VH1 placed *Strange Days* at #60 on its list of top albums. The same year, *L.A. Woman* placed at #362 on *Rolling Stone*'s 500 Greatest Albums of All Time. In 2004, *Rolling Stone* magazine ranked the Doors #41 on their list of the 100 Greatest Artists of All Time.

Two years later, a box set of the Doors' studio recordings was released, and a coffee-table book, *The Doors by the Doors*, was published. Production also began on an officially sanctioned documentary of the group's history. And to top it all off, the Doors were awarded a lifetime achievement award at the 2007 Grammy Awards (along with the Grateful Dead and Joan Baez, another two rock legends from the sixties). In February 2007, the Doors also received a star on the Hollywood Walk of Fame.

That same month, Ian Astbury decided to quit Riders on the Storm, as he was planning to relaunch his old band, the Cult. Brett Scallions, former lead singer of Fuel, took his place as frontman for Riders on the Storm.

Meanwhile, a new generation is listening to the Doors. In an article in *Word*, Ray explained why their music is still relevant:

> "It's clean, it's pure—there is a keyboard on one side, a guitar on the other, drums in the middle, a bassline underneath that and the singer up front—*and* you can hear the words. That's one of the reasons why the Doors sound is still important today. It's perfectly modern. That's what we wanted."

When the Doors first became popular, it was the underground counterculture that were their biggest fans. Along the way, these fans may have been disappointed in some of the directions the Doors chose to take, but today, there is still a healthy underground market for Doors music. Many bootleg recordings continue to circulate, including ones of the group's 1967 and 1968 concerts, especially two concerts that took place in Stockholm, Sweden. The infamous Miami show is also available, as well as the *Rock Is Dead* studio jam from 1969. The Doors' message is still singing—and people are still listening.

Open Doors

So what is the message that the Doors has to offer today? Certainly not that psychedelic drugs are the answer to the world's problems. Jim Morrison's life—and many other lives from his era—proved these drugs didn't offer the freedom they promised; instead, addiction turned out to be just another destructive trap.

But while the sixties' drugs, free sex, and out-of-control antics may no longer seem very relevant to the twenty-first–century world, the Doors' music still speaks to something deep inside many of us.

Jim said:

> "I offer images—I conjure memories of freedom that can still be reached—like the Doors, right? But we can only open the doors, we can't drag people through. I can't free them unless they want to be free. Maybe primitive people have less [stuff] to let go of, to give up. A person has to be willing to give up everything—not just wealth. All the [stuff] that he's been taught—all society's brainwashing. You have to let go of all that to get to the other side. Most people aren't willing to do that."

After Jim

Jim Morrison was possibly one of the most talented songwriters and vocalists of the 1960s and early 1970s. Just how far he and the Doors could have gone will never be known. Like many people of the time, drugs and alcohol destroyed the musician's life, cutting it short and depriving the world of a true legend.

Like another great teacher, Jesus of Nazareth, Jim spoke of doors in our hearts that only we can open; like the Buddha, Jim knew that when we let go of the material world, we find a deeper reality. Like all the great mystics, Jim believed that spiritual reality is important to everyday life. The images he offered with his words, words that the Doors brought to life with their music, continue to challenge us all to seek our freedom in that deeper realm.

CHRONOLOGY

1965 Jim Morrison and Ray Manzarek meet and form a band.

1966 The group plays at the London Fog and the Whisky a Go Go.

August 18 The Doors sign a contract with Elektra Records.

August 21 The Doors are fired from the Whisky a Go Go following a crude performance by Jim.

1967 *The Doors*, the group's first album, is released.

April "Light My Fire" is released, propelling the Doors to the top of the record charts.

September 17 The Doors make their first appearance on *The Ed Sullivan Show*.

December 10 Jim is arrested in New Haven, Connecticut.

December 26–28 The Doors perform at San Francisco's Winterland Ballroom.

December 30–31 The Doors close out the year with performances in Denver, Colorado.

1968 *Waiting for the Sun* becomes the group's first #1 album.

February *Rolling Stone* criticizes the staged antics of the Doors' performances.

May The Doors play at Chicago Coliseum, where police had to be called to handle the crowd.

June "Hello, I Love You" becomes the group's last #1 single.

September Jim goes to London to recover from a drug binge.

1969 **January 24** The Doors play a sold-out concert at Madison Square Garden.

February The Doors hold the famous "Rock Is Dead" jam sessions.

March 1 Jim's late arrival for a Miami, Florida, concert causes crowd unrest; during the performance, he exposes himself and is arrested.

April Jim begins filming *HWY*, in which he played the lead.

June and July A bluesier Doors perform in Chicago and Hollywood.

November Jim is arrested for being abusive to flight attendants during a flight to Phoenix; he is eventually acquitted.

CHRONOLOGY

1970 **August** The group performs at the Isle of Wight Festival.

September Jim is found guilty of indecent exposure and profanity in the Miami incident.

1971 **March** Jim and his girlfriend move to Paris.

July 3 Jim Morrison dies in Paris.

1972 The surviving Doors stop recording and performing.

1978 The surviving Doors put music to Jim's poetry and release *An American Prayer*.

1979 "The End" is used in the sound track of *Apocalypse Now*.

1991 *The Doors* film is released.

1993 The Doors are inducted into the Rock and Roll Hall of Fame.

1998 *Q* magazine ranks *Strange Days* #93 on the list of Greatest Albums of All Times.

2000 The remaining Doors create Bright Midnight Records.

2002 Ray and Robby form Doors of the 21st Century.

Rolling Stone ranks *Strange Days* #42 on its list of 500 Greatest Albums of All Time.

2003 **February** John files suit to make Ray and Robby stop using the name "Doors."

Rolling Stone ranks *L.A. Woman* #362 on its list of the 500 Greatest Albums of All Time, and VH1 places *Strange Days* at #60 on its list of top albums.

2004 *Rolling Stone* ranks the Doors #41 on its list of the 100 Greatest Artists of All Time.

2005 The band is forced to change its name; they choose D21C; they now perform as Riders on the Storm.

2006 **November 8** Ray Manzarek and Robby Krieger perform at the Whisky a Go Go to celebrate the fortieth anniversary of the Doors.

2007 The Doors receive a Grammy Award Lifetime Achievement Award and a star on the Hollywood Walk of Fame.

ACCOMPLISHMENTS & AWARDS

Albums

1967   *The Doors*
        Strange Days

1968   *Waiting for the Sun*

1969   *The Soft Parade*

1970   *Absolutely Alive*
        Morrison Hotel
        13

1971   *L.A. Woman*
        Other Voices

1972   *Full Circle*
        Weird Scenes Inside the Gold Mine

1978   *An American Prayer: Jim Morrison*

1980   *Alive, She Cried*

1987   *Live at the Hollywood Bowl*

1996   *The Doors Greatest Hits*

1999   *Complete Studio Recordings*

2003   *Legacy: The Absolute Best*

2004   *Live in Detroit*

2006   *Perception*

Number-One Singles

1967   "Light My Fire"

1968   "Hello, I Love You"

Videos

1991   *The Doors Live in Europe*

1999   *The Doors Collection*

2002   *Doors Are Open*
        Doors—Soundstage Performances
        No One Here Gets Out Alive—The Doors' Tribute to
           Jim Morrison

ACCOMPLISHMENTS & AWARDS

2005 *Inside the Doors 1967–1969: A Critical Review*

2006 *Doors: Total Rock Review*

Book

2006 The Doors and Ben Fong-Torres. *The Doors.* New York: Hyperion.

Awards/Recognitions

1993 The Doors are inducted into the Rock and Roll Hall of Fame.

1998 Q magazine: *Strange Days* is ranked #93 on the list of Greatest Albums of All Times

2002 *Rolling Stone*: *Strange Days* is ranked #42 on its list of 500 Greatest Albums of All Time.

2003 *Rolling Stone*: *L.A. Woman* is ranked #362 on its list of the 500 Greatest Albums of All Time.

VH1: *Strange Days* is ranked #60 on its list of top albums.

2004 *Rolling Stone*: The Doors are ranked #41 on its list of the 100 Greatest Artists of All Time.

2007 Grammy Awards: The Doors receive a Lifetime Achievement Award.

The group receives a star on the Hollywood Walk of Fame.

FURTHER READING & INTERNET RESOURCES

Books

Densmore, John. *Riders on the Storm: My Life with Jim Morrison and the Doors.* New York: Delta, 1991.

The Doors and Ben Fong-Torres. *The Doors.* New York: Hyperion, 2006.

Hopkins, Jerry, and Danny Sugerman. *No One Here Gets Out Alive.* New York: Warner Books, 2006.

Manzarek, Ray. *Light My Fire.* New York: Berkley Trade, 1999.

Morrison, Jim. *Lords and New Creatures.* New York: Fireside, 1971.

Morrison, Jim. *Wilderness: The Lost Writings of Jim Morrison.* New York: Vintage, 1989.

Morrison, Jim. *The American Night: The Writings of Jim Morrison.* New York: Vintage, 1991.

Web Sites

www.johndensmore.com
John Densmore—Official Web Site

www.raymanzarek.us
Ray Manzarek—Official Web Site

www.robbykrieger.com
Robby Krieger—Official Web Site

www.rockhall.com
Rock and Roll Hall of Fame

www.thedoors.com
The Doors

GLOSSARY

acquitted—Found officially not guilty of a charge or accusation.

blues—Popular music that developed from African American folk songs in the early twentieth century.

bootleg—Something illegally made.

commercialism—Excessive emphasis on making a profit.

controversial—Provoking strong disagreement or disapproval.

cover—A new version of a song made popular by another performer.

cynicism—Having a distrust of human nature.

inducted—Formally admitted into an organization.

inhibitions—Feelings or beliefs that prevent someone from behaving spontaneously or speaking freely.

mescaline—A mind-altering drug that comes from the button-shaped nodules on the stem of the peyote plant.

mystical—Having a spiritual meaning and reality that is neither apparent to the five senses nor obvious to rational intelligence.

perverse—Purposely deviating from what is accepted as good or proper.

prestigious—Much admired and respected.

psychedelic—Relating to the effects of mind-altering drugs.

R&B—Rhythm and blues; a style of music that combines elements of blues and jazz.

sociopath—An person with a personality disorder characterized by antisocial thoughts and behaviors.

underground—Separate from the mainstream establishment, having to do especially with an experimental social or artistic environment.

venue—Location for an event.

INDEX

"Alabama Song" (song), 21
alcohol, 27, 29, 55
Alive, She Cried (album), 46
An American Prayer (poem single), 46
Astbury, Ian (singer), 49, 50, 53

"Back Door Man" (song), 21
Boot Yer But (CD set), 48
"Break on Through" (song), 21, 50
Britain, 30, 31
"Build Me a Woman" (song), 37

California, 10, 14, 15, 33
CBS, 23, 24
"Celebration of the Lizard" (song), 29
Coppola, Francis Ford (director), 46, 47
Courson, Pamela (girlfriend of Jim Morrison), 40, 41, 47, 50

Davis, Stephen (author), 26
Densmore, John
  and beginning of the Doors, 16
  and death of Jim Morrison, 44
  present day, 49, 50, 51, 53
The Doors
  after Jim Morrison, 45–50
  disagreements between members, 50–54
  finding fame, 21–31
  formation, 14–19
  fortieth anniversary, 9–13
  and problems with Jim Morrison, 31–41
The Doors (album), 21
The Doors (movie), 46
The Doors of Perception (book), 16

The Ed Sullivan Show (TV show), 22, 23, 24
Elektra Records, 19, 20, 21, 28
"The End" (song), 21

Full Circle (album), 45

Grammy Awards, 52, 53

"Hello, I Love You" (song), 29, 31
Hendrix, Jimi (singer), 10, 38
The History of Rock (book), 39
Hollywood, 9, 37, 52, 53
Huxley, Aldous (author), 16
HWY (film), 35

"I Will Never Be Untrue" (song), 37

Jonathan Winters Show (TV show), 25, 26

Kilmer, Val (actor), 46, 47
Krieger, Robby
  and beginning of the Doors, 16
  and death of Jim Morrison, 44
  at fortieth anniversary of the Doors, 8, 9, 11
  and Hollywood Walk of Fame, 52
  present day, 48, 49, 50, 51

L.A. Woman (album), 40
"Light My Fire" (song), 19, 22, 23, 25
"Love Me Two Times" (song), 26
"Love Her Madly" (song), 40

ABOUT THE AUTHOR

Rae Simons is the author of many young adult books. She lives in upstate New York with a small menagerie of animals. She has always been a Doors fan and remembers clearly the first time she heard "Riders on the Storm" when she was twelve years old.

Picture Credits

page

- **2:** Elektra Records/Star Photos
- **8:** RW3/WENN Photos
- **11:** Hector Mata/AFP/Getty Images
- **12:** Giulio Marcocchi/Sipa Press
- **14:** Elektra Records/Star Photos
- **17:** Rare Pics Int'l
- **18:** Foto Feature Collection
- **20:** Elektra Records/Star Photos
- **23:** Foto Feature Collection
- **25:** UPI Photo Archive
- **27:** Foto Feature Collection
- **28:** Elektra Records/Star Photos
- **30:** Central Press/Mirrorpix
- **32:** Elektra Records/Star Photos
- **35:** UPI Photo Archive
- **36:** Foto Feature Collection
- **39:** New Millennium Images
- **40:** Starstock/Photoshot
- **42:** New Millennium Images
- **44:** Foto Feature Collection
- **47:** Tri-Star Pictures/NMI
- **49:** New Millennium Images
- **51:** Giulio Marcocchi/Sipa Press
- **52:** Russell Einhorn/Splash News
- **55:** Elektra Records/Star Photos

Front cover: Elektra Records/Star Photos

INDEX

Madison Square Garden, 33
Manzarek, Ray, 11, 13, 20, 21, 26, 37
  and beginning of the Doors, 14, 15, 16, 17, 18, 19
  and death of Jim Morrison, 44
  at fortieth anniversary of the Doors, 8, 9, 11
  and Hollywood Walk of Fame, 52
  in band after Jim Morrison, 45
  present day, 48, 49, 50, 51, 52, 53
Miami, Florida, 34, 35, 38, 54
"Moonlight Drive" (song), 16, 25
Morrison, Jim
  and beginning of the Doors, 14, 15, 16, 17
  death, 12, 41, 42, 44, 45
  and drugs, 16, 27, 29, 30, 31, 34, 37, 38, 40
  legal problems, 24, 25, 34, 38, 41
  rebellion, 19, 24, 32, 42, 43
Morrison Hotel (album), 38

"Not to Touch the Earth" (song), 29

Other Voices (album), 45

"People Are Strange" (song), 26
Perception (box set), 48

"Riders on the Storm" (song), 40
Riders on the Storm (band), 50, 53

rock
  music, 18, 24, 53
  singers, 11, 14, 16, 18, 19, 22, 34, 39, 53
Rock and Roll Hall of Fame, 8, 48
Rock Encyclopedia (book), 29
Rock is Dead (studio jam), 34, 54
Rolling Stone (magazine), 26, 53
Rolling Stones, 38
Roxon, Lillian (author), 29

Scallions, Brett (singer), 53
The Soft Parade (album), 37
Strange Days (album), 26, 48, 53
Sugarman, Danny (author), 41, 42, 48

"Touch Me" (song), 33, 37
The Doors of the 21st Century (band), 49, 50

UCLA, 15, 46
"Unknown Soldier" (song), 29

Waiting for the Sun (album), 28, 29, 31
Whisky a Go Go club, 9, 10, 19
The Who, 10, 38
"Who Do You Love?" (song), 37
Wonderland Avenue (book), 41, 42